The First Bengali Novel (1868) penned by a Woman

Manottama

Narrative of a Sorrowful Wife

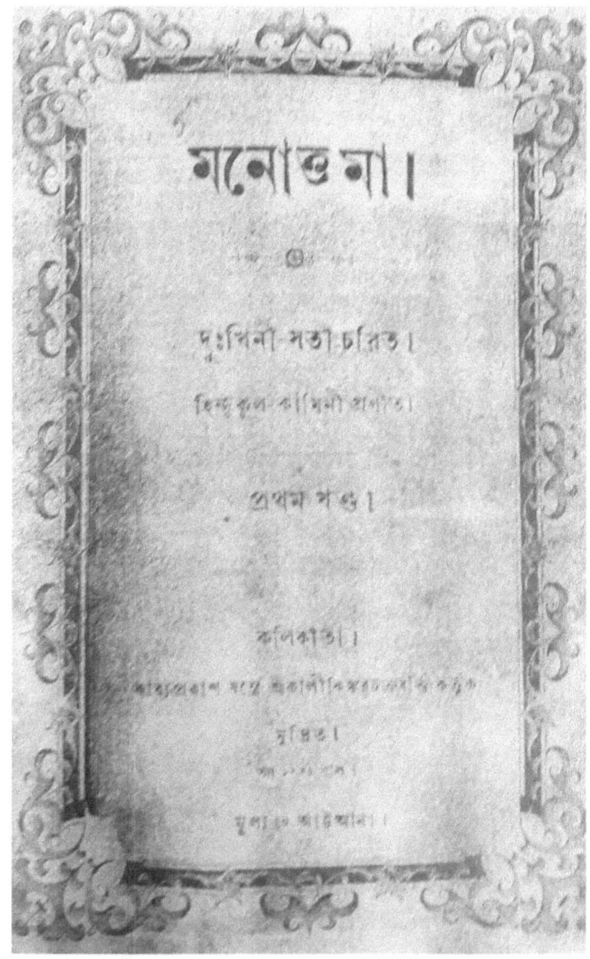

Opening page of the original Bengali book first published in Kolkata by Sri Kalikinkar Chakrabarti in 1275 B.E. and priced at eight annas.

The First Bengali Novel (1868) penned by a Woman

Manottama
[Dukkhini Sati Charit]

Narrative of a Sorrowful Wife

Anonymous
Hindukula-Kamini Pranito
(by a woman belonging to the Hindu lineage)

Introduced and translated
from the original Bengali by
Somdatta Mandal

Foreword by **Rosinka Chaudhuri**

Shambhabi
THE THIRD EYE IMPRINT
NEW DELHI | CALCUTTA

SHAMBHABI THE THIRD EYE IMPRINT
70-B/9 Amritpuri, East of Kailash, New Delhi 65
33/1/2 K B Sarani, Mall Road, Calcutta 80

Email: thethirdeyeimprint@gmail.com
Website: www.hawakal.com

Cover designed by Bitan Chakraborty

First edition April 2021

ISBN: 978-81-948077-8-0 (Paperback)

ISBN: 978-81-948077-7-3 (Hardbound)

Copyright 2021 © Somdatta Mandal

All rights reserved. No part of this publication may be reproduced or transmitted (other than for purposes of review or critique) in any form or by any means, electronic or mechanical, including photocopy, recording, or any information storage and retrieval system without prior permission in writing from the publisher and the translator where applicable.

Price: INR 300 | USD 14.99

Distributed by HAWAKAL PUBLISHERS

Manottama
A SIGNIFICANT TEXT IN ITS TIME

Manottama, written by somebody describing herself as a 'Hindukula Kamini' [A Hindu Woman], was published in colonial Calcutta in 1868. Ten years before this, in an amazing coincidence not widely celebrated by the Bengali reading public, modern Bengali literature in all three of its main genres — poetry, drama, and fiction — had been self-consciously generated by a handful of men in 1858. Rangalal Bandyopadhyay had published his long verse narrative with India's first modern literary manifesto preceding it, the *Padmini upākhyān*, in 1858; Pearychand Mittra published the first Bengali novel in book form, *Ālāler ghare dulāl*, in 1858; and Madhusudan Datta inaugurated his career in Bengali by writing a modern Bengali play, *Sharmisthā nātak*, in 1858 — this was subsequently published in January 1859. This was a time when older forms were beginning to be discarded or refashioned for being inadequate to the requirements of the modern age, a time which therefore soon saw newer constituencies, such as women, join the race to be part of this new modernity.

The story of the text's retrieval from the archives in Britain in 2010 by Adrish Biswas — given by Somdatta Mandal in her introduction — is dramatic and vivid testimony to the excitements of archival research. Prof. Mandal has translated and introduced *Manottama* for the first time to English-speaking readers now, and she has given a detailed list of other women writers and their publications at this time. From it we may observe that this was a period fecund with productions from the pens of women — many pioneering efforts by them were published in the sixth and seventh decades of the nineteenth century, each as significant as the other. It was also a time when the world was superficially divided into inner and outer domains, with the inner domestic sphere firmly the place of women, and the outer professional or worldly sphere that of men. Yet no such binary should be accepted without caution, as inner and outer mingle remarkably in the conscious experience and the everyday, as well as in language and literature. If the office-goer in colonial Calcutta was negotiating the disciplinary regime of the city, then the domestic sphere he belonged to was no less oriented by the timetable of office hours on office days and leisure hours on holidays. Equally, while the subject matter of *Manottoma* may predictably dwell in the domestic sphere, and is constructed as a woman's advice to other women, on the other hand, women at this time were not just shown in the kitchen or the house in literary works — Bankimchandra Chatterjee's *Durgeshnandini* (1865) and *Kapalkundala* (1866) both depicted the most unusual of women in the most unusual of circumstances, untied down by domesticity.

The education and liberation of women had been an important subject in nineteenth-century Bengal's intellectual circles for some time before this. The concerted efforts of like-minded social reformers like Ramgopal Ghosh, Dakshinaranjan Mukherjee and Madan Mohan Tarkalankar had seen John Drinkwater Elliot Bethune establish Calcutta's first school for girls in 1849 called the Hindu Female School, later known as Bethune School. By 1878, just a decade after *Manottama* was published, Bethune School had sent up the first woman candidate for the Entrance Examination at the University of Calcutta, Kadambini Ganguly (nee Basu), who went on to become one of India's first women doctors. Notwithstanding these pioneering achievements in women's education at this time, however, the archetype of the ideal woman as mother, wife, and homemaker remained a powerful idea in nineteenth-century society. In *Manottama*, we see both strands exist simultaneously and conflictedly in a narrative that both privileges education for women as well as shows us how that education, in fact, could result in the production of an ideal wife, mother and homemaker.

When Radhanath Sikdar and Pearychand Mittra had inaugurated and edited a magazine for women called the *Masik Patrika* in 1857 upward of a decade before *Manottama* was written, they had proclaimed:

> *Ei patrikā sādhāraner bisheshatah strīloker janya chhāpā haitechhe, je bhāshāy āmāder sacharāchar kathābārtā hoy, tāhātei prastāb sakal rachanā haibek. Bignya panditerā parite chān, pariben, kintu tāhādiger nimitte ei patrikā likhita hoy nāi.*

> [This magazine is being published for the ordinary person, particularly women, in the language in which we routinely converse – all the articles will be written in this style. If the intellectuals and the pandits wish to read it, they may, but this magazine is not being written for them.]

Masik Patrika went on to serialize Pearychand's *Alaler Ghare Dulal* [which he claimed was 'an original Novel in Bengali being the first work of its kind'] which told the dire story of the perils of spoiling a child. Permeated through and through by a vigorous

IV

didacticism, it was written in a similar style and with a similar purpose as the current text under discussion, *Manottama*, with which it shares its linguistic style, its didacticism, and its serialization in a magazine (a common enough occurrence at the time). Both texts also share the format of the moral tale, where the binary of good and evil divides the characters clearly and unambiguously. No stylistic clues exist within the text to allow us to decide whether the text had actually been written by a man or woman; although Adrish Biswas traced the evidence to colonial police catalogues that recorded the text as having been written by a 'Kamini Devi', the generic nature of the name and lack of biographical and other details leave us in a state of uncertainty till such time as more information may emerge from the efforts of future researchers.

Manottama begins, interestingly enough, by claiming to be 'a history.' When the generically-named friends Jadav and Madhav sit together on a moonlit night in spring, the former says to the latter: '*Mitra! Bahu din itihas shuni nāi, adya ekti itihās shunite bāsanā haitechhe*' the word '*itihas*,' translated here quite correctly as 'historical tale,' testifies to the implied facticity of the story about to unfold. Stylistically, one of the first things to note is the absence of inverted commas or spacing of any kind to indicate dialogue, so that when Madhav agrees to the proposition, in the Bengali text the sentence simply runs on: '*Madhav kahilen, bandhu! Galpati ati dīrgha, jadi birakta nā how, sraban kara.*' This is perhaps what Prof. Mandal has in mind when she speaks of the traditional style of the text, and she is right not to adhere to the original now archaic style and instead insert the customary inverted commas and capitalization around 'Friend! The story is very long. If you don't feel bored, listen to it.'

The story in actuality is not very long. There is also very little chance of feeling bored while listening to it or reading it. An important text in the history of Bengali modernity, *Manottama* deserves to be read and appreciated for its significance in time, as a marker of the development not so much of women's right to equality or parity but as an argument, an opinion, a perspective on the good that education can do for a woman in her life and the life of those around her. It may not be an argument one would agree with in this day and age, but it is one that needs to be studied as representative of an age and a period that was instrumental in our making.

Rosinka Chaudhuri
Director & Professor of Cultural Studies
The Centre for Studies in Social Sciences, Calcutta

INTRODUCTION

Somdatta Mandal

I: Historicizing the Text

A brief survey of the rise of the Bengali novel in the nineteenth century shows that although Peary Chand Mittra's *Alaler Ghare Dulal* (1854) may lay claim to it, it was in fact Bankimchandra Chattopadhyay's *Durgeshnandini,* published in 1865, that is accepted by the general public as the first proper Bengali novel, followed by his *Kapalkundala* in 1866. As we are aware, Bankimchandra had borrowed the literary genre of the novel from the British and accordingly wrote his first novel *Rajmohan's Wife* in English in

11

1864. But soon he switched over to Bengali and the novel form flourished under his stewardship for several years. Interestingly enough, during the same period writing novels in Bengali by women also went on simultaneously, though literary historians did not elaborate on them. None of the reputed scholars like Srikumar Bandyopadhyay, Sisirkumar Das or Sukumar Sen in their books on the history of the Bengali novel clearly mention who the pioneer in the field of women's writing actually was. In his treatise *Bangla Sahityer Itihas,* Vol. 3, Sukumar Sen gives us a list of thirteen novels written by women which somehow emulate Bankimchandra's novels that began after the publication of *Durgeshnandini* and went on till the publication of *Bishbriksha,* and in that list the anonymous *Manottama* holds the second position. The novels were written on diverse subjects ranging from educational texts to moral tales, from romantic or historical adventures to love stories.

There are several alternative claims for the position of the first Bengali woman novelist. Hemangini Devi wrote *Manorama* in 1865 but published it in 1874. *Manottama* by a 'Hindukula Kamini' (anonymous, mentioning it as a novel written by 'A Woman of the Hindu Lineage') was published in 1868, *Kaminikalanka* by Nabinkali Devi in 1870, *Tarabati* by Shibsundari Devi in 1873, *Deepnirban* by Swarnakumari Devi in 1876 (published anonymously), and later *Malati* (1880), *Snehalata* (1892) and *Kahake*

(1898) also by her, are some of the significant titles. Speaking about women's writing and anonymity, it needs to be reiterated that writing under a pseudonym or not mentioning the name at all were very common prevalent devices of the time. Adrish Biswas in his introduction to his edited version of *Manottama* (Ananda Publishers, 2011) mentions that a detailed search from 1868 to 1900 for novels written by Bengali women resulted in 37 entries, out of which 7 were anonymous.

Incidentally, the practice of writing and anonymously publishing women's creative works was not only restricted to the genre of the novel. Around the same time when so many novels were being published in the late 19th century, we also come across *Kaminee: The Virgin Widow* (1874), an anonymously published play which relates the fate of an accomplished teenage widow in Calcutta when the Hindu Widows' Remarriage Act has become law, yet most people paid no heed to it. This Act, implemented in 1856, legalised the remarriage of Hindu widows in all jurisdictions of India under the rule of the East India Company. Since the play was written in English, we are of course not sure whether the anonymous playwright was male or female. Two years later, in 1876, Rashosundari Devi published her autobiography, *Amar Jibon*, which is a landmark document of women's domesticity and the struggles and pitfalls of education at that point of time. That very same year also saw the publication of Nawab

Faizunnesa Chaudhurani's famous literary text *Rupjalal* that was published from Dhaka and it was the first ever book to be authored in Bengali by a Muslim lady. It challenged established notions regarding women's position in a Muslim society in colonial Bengal. This love story was not written in direct prose but in a combination of poetry and prose form called 'champu,' but it broke the false notion of the educated Hindu society that Muslim women could not write well. Women's education and female emancipation were also important agenda of the Brahmo Samaj during this time. Begum Rokeya's novel *Sultana's Dream* which dreamt of a utopian state where women controlled everything including ruling the state and men were kept at home in the 'mardana' was written in English and published much later in 1905. So, the timing of writing the anonymous novel *Manottama* is significant because it gives us a typical Hindu conservative householder's point of view and though structurally weak, it also gives us a detailed picture of contemporary society with all its superstitions and pitfalls. In a rather preaching tone, it goes on reiterating the fact that a married woman's place is beside her husband, however undeserving he might be. If not a superb novel, at least it is an honest attempt by a Bengali woman to write a novel in the Bengali language dwhich has not received the attention it deserves.

II: Locating the Text

The credit for rescuing the text from oblivion rests entirely upon the late scholar Adrish Biswas who managed to retrieve it from the archives of the British Library in London as late as 2010. The story of that recovery is quite interesting. As a research scholar in nineteenth-century popular literature, Biswas received a Charles Wallace Trust Fellowship to visit the British Library in London. He had heard that the only copy of *Manottama* was kept there. He searched the catalogue but there was no book by that name. He told the person who was in charge that he had heard that the first women's novel written in Bangla was there but he couldn't find it in the catalogue. He showed a keen interest to recover that text and take it back to his country because it had a remarkable significance in the history of Bengali literature and therefore was a treasure.

The person in the library to whom Biswas mentioned this was not a Bengali. So, it was not expected that he would have any responsibility for it. But one had to learn from the British the meaning of cooperation and preservation. He told him that there were some 'rare' books of about twenty-four volumes but he did not know what was inside them but he could have a look. Biswas agreed. But since the books were very rare, they were specially preserved in the British Museum. If he put in a request on one day, the books would come the next day. Biswas then applied to have a look at all the twenty-four volumes. Just because no one knew what was inside the books, there was no catalogue. It was highly appreciable that for people who did not know the language, the books were preserved so beautifully. That is why the books also receive Z-plus security like the members of the royal household.

So, the following day the books arrived in a big van along with policemen with rifles in the pilot cars before and after the vehicle. It was really an astonishing sight. They brought all the twenty-four volumes for Biswas to go through. Each lot had twenty books per volume but none of them had any catalogue. Why was it so? Since they were rare books they could be stolen or looted and hence were left without any catalogue. Biswas picked up each volume and turned the pages but he could not find *Manottama*. He went on searching till suddenly he found one book with the broken 19th century lead type where the name *Manottama* was written. His happiness knew no bounds and he photocopied the whole book. After that the books went back to the British Museum once again under Z-plus security.

After returning to India, Biswas started researching on the book. The novel was written under a pseudonym – "Hindu Kula Kamini pranito" ['Written by a Woman of the Hindu lineage']. The year was 1868. Who was this Hindu lady? He did not know. Was it published earlier? After crossing several hurdles, Biswas started going through the advertisements in various nineteenth century journals. He found the name of *Nabaprabandha* journal and in 1867 the novel was published in instalments for almost a year in this monthly periodical under the title *Manottama*. There was no name of the editor, only the name of the printer stated 'Published by Tincurry Ghosul" from 149 Maniktala Street, Calcutta.' Biswas then worked very hard to find the whereabouts of the writer. This was because there was no mention about her in any reference book. Even scholars like Sukumar Sen and others who wrote about the rise and development of the Bengali novel did not provide any information about the name of the first woman novelist or the name of the work.

In the end Biswas located a catalogue from the police where the name of *Manottama* was mentioned and the author as Kamini Devi residing in Hooghly. Five hundred copies of the book had been printed and that information was also noted there. Now the question arises why the police got hold of such a catalogue. During the British rule there was a great revolution. Many Bengali intellectuals supported it but the British intelligence was unable to locate them. In order to keep everything under surveillance, the British made a law that two copies of all published books should be given to them. They would then go through the book to see whether there was any seditious content or idea of revolution in it. And then they made a catalogue of these books. Out of the two copies, they kept one set here and the other one was taken to their country. That was how a copy of the book *Manottama* was stored in the British Library and Museum. It was a strange collection and Biswas was greatly impressed by the glorious manner in which they had preserved it. Thus, *Manottama* edited by Adrish Biswas was ultimately published by Ananda Publishers in Kolkata in 2011. It is unfortunate that even today this important novel has not received the attention it deserves from scholars and general readers alike.

III: About the Text

As mentioned earlier, *Manottama* the novel, published in book form in 1868, was published serially for almost a year beginning from September 1866 in a new journal called *Nabaprabandha*. The sub-title of the novel 'Dukhini Sati Charit' meaning the 'Narrative of a Sorrowful Wife' is a clear pointer to the plight of women in contemporary society at the time. Also, the anonymous author calling it "Hindu Kulakamini Pranito" or 'Written by a Woman of the Hindu Lineage' makes it clear that it is going to be a 'slice of life' picture painted by a Hindu woman of the time. During that period many journals did not even publish the name of the writers. The story of this novel was totally different. The name of 'Manottama' in the novel was also the name of the protagonist. So, it can be said that this book was simultaneously written by a woman and it was the story of a woman. As a young girl Manottama was brought up and educated by her father. The message conveyed by this first Bengali novel written by a woman is that there is a lot of value in being educated. After she grew up, eventually the educated Manottama got married to an uneducated man. This was unusual – although in *Jogajog* Rabindranath depicted an educated and refined woman being married to an unrefined businessman, it was certainly not the norm. In nineteenth-century society, even in its fiction, men were educated much before women and after that they would marry uneducated women and then give them education. There are several examples beginning from Kailashbasini Devi to the various marriages that took place in the Tagore household and there are such examples in literature as well.

But Manottama narrates a different story to us. What was that? She started educating her husband Nilabrata and that hurt his prestige. So, according to the advice of two of his friends and in order to teach her a lesson, he went and married for a second time. But Manottama did not revolt and leave the house. She went on staying at her in-law's place and tried to solve the new problem through education. Education gave her the strength to combat all the problems in her household but more importantly, it taught her the values of patience and endurance. She started teaching the children of the new wife and her 'enlightened' weapon became effective. This new method of regaining respect in the Indian, especially Hindu tradition was totally new but we did not know about this feature of Indian society. Much later stories and novels were written about liberated and enlightened women protagonists. But that it had already taken place in the very first novel itself, was beyond our knowledge. As a result, though written in the flowery language of formal Bengali to a large extent, with several sections elaborately justifying the didactic motive of the author, *Manottama* surprises us in various aspects.

As mentioned earlier, structurally the novel is quite weak as the main purpose of the novelist is to impart the dogma that education raises the mental strength of a woman to such an extent that she is able to withstand all the problems of her domestic life with equanimity. Like the other characters who are painted in either black and white, Manottama is made the epitome of virtue who possesses all the ideal feminine qualities. Throughout the story she is contrasted with Bimalprabha, the co-wife, who is once again evil in all respects. Though unbelievable at times, she always speaks in a polite and sweet voice and treats her own children and those of her co-wife equally, and not once in the story do we find her retorting or reacting to any incident with a strong voice Sof protest. Even when her husband kicks her and misbehaves with her on several occasions, she still remains quiet and nonplussed. Whether this was the right thing to do is never questioned by the author. Throughout the entire text she goes on narrating the incidents through the binary of good versus evil.

One interesting section of the story offers a detailed picture of contemporary Hindu society with all its caste and class ridden problems where we are shown how the so-called heads of various factions or self-styled social leaders claimed to change the traditional and established rules as and according to their own convenience. This comes out clearly when Nilabrata makes elaborate arrangements to celebrate his son's *annaprasan* or rice-eating ceremony and almost all the social leaders arrive there and expose their jealousy, hatred, shrewdness with most of them having a personal axe to grind. Among the other issues of quarrel and conflict, they unanimously protest on four issues, namely, widow remarriage, educating the girl child, not accepting the status of the daughter's marriage if not given in a *kulin* household, and not getting a son married by the age of sixteen. They considered all these issues as great deviation from the religion and were actually steps leading to sin. In another section the author also digresses and tells us about how the British who were uncivilized were now ruling the Indians in Bharatvarsha, a country which has a much more ancient tradition and civilization.

Towards the end of the novella we are convinced that the author's main intention was to preach and impart the lesson that whatever might happen, a woman's place is in her husband's home. When her father Yogananda comes to visit Manottama and asks her to go and stay with him for some time because they were still debt-ridden and passing through difficult financial conditions, Manottama flatly refuses to do so. Instead, she gives us (and the contemporary readers of her story) ample instances from the ancient epics and folklores of women who withstood all the hardship in life but never deserted their husbands. She gives individual examples of Sita, Savitri, Damayanti, Chinta, Draupadi, and even Fullara, who belonged to a lower caste, to prove that down the ages, none of these women had ever left their husband's company even during very difficult times. Thus, they provided perfect examples of ideal womanhood.

The novella ends quite abruptly without any total resolution of the problems in the typical 'and they lived happily ever after' manner. The words "End of the first section" mentioned at the end of the story offer clear indication that the author probably had the desire to continue the story further but no such text has yet been located. In its extant state therefore, in spite of its drawbacks, *Manottama* still remains a good example of a picture of contemporary Hindu society of the time which was still debating between old, traditional ideas and the new progressive ones. Leaving aside the anonymity of the author, the issues discussed in the novel deserve more attention in the present times.

Manottama

Narrative of a Sorrowful Wife

art credit wikipedia

Manottama

Once upon a time on a night before the full moon in spring, two friends called Jadav and Madhav were sitting in a wide courtyard. Jadav said, "Friend! I haven't heard a historical tale for a long time, and today I desire to listen to one. You have the capability of narrating stories quite well. Since I find you have some leisure time today, and if you feel that abiding by my request will not be inconvenient for you, please make me happy by narrating the story of Manottama."

Madhav said, "Friend! The story is very long. If you don't feel bored, listen to it." Saying that, he began to narrate the story.

In an eastern land there was a businessman called Nilabrata who would squander away his money. He did not receive the required education while his father was present. This was why no one agreed to marry him. His father had a friend called Yogananda who lived in the same village and was in the same business. Yogananda was well-educated and he had an unmarried daughter who was also well-educated. Her name was Manottama.

One day Yogananda went to Nilabrata's residence with a marriage proposal. He requested Nilabrata to accept his daughter. Nilabrata said, "Sir, you are my father's friend, so I should not disobey your order. But just consider the fact that I am already over forty years of age and your daughter is a child, hardly above the age of nine. Under such circumstances it is not logical for you to make such a request and so I am in a way disapproving your proposal. Please pardon me in this matter. Instead let me look for a good and young bridegroom and will get your daughter married. But I myself cannot agree to marry a teenage girl like her. Seeing his reluctance for marriage, Yogananda started offering a lot of advice to Nilabrata. Nilabrata himself was not that educated but he had heard from people that one should not marry a young girl and so he had refused the proposal. But at the very next moment Dnt his desire to get married became so strong in his heart that he gave his consent to Yogananda. After that both of them arrived at Yogananda's house and by undergoing all the rituals according to the *Kulin* tradition, the marriage of Manottama with Nilabrata took place on an auspicious day. But after accepting Nilabrata as her husband, Yogananda's daughter did not feel contented with conjugal bliss. This incompatibility did not arise because she was a young girl. By nature, Nilabrata was uneducated and ill-natured; Manottama was by nature educated and docile. Thus, instead of developing mental compatibility among themselves, they gradually drifted apart in reverse directions. Therefore, for six or seven years they spent their time in continuous mental tension. Each night Manottama would get hold of a couple of charming books and read them aloud to her husband. On some days Nilabrata would get annoyed with that and leave the house; on other days he would rebuke his wife and would go and sleep in another house. He would blame himself of the wrong deed he had committed by marrying this ill-natured woman. He should have stuck to his decision expressed to her father of not agreeing to marry her. Instead, he committed this great sin without thinking about the pros and cons. He would sometimes express these feelings to his friends and prostitutes.

Alas! There can be no end to saying how dissatisfying and troublesome an intelligent and educated woman can be for an uneducated man. Seeing his behaviour, Manottama decided she would no longer become the trouble-maker of her husband by reading out from books;

27

henceforth whenever her husband returned home, she would spend her time in ordinary conversation. Why should she go against religion by doing deeds that were disliked by her husband? Thinking about this she would sometimes turn morose. Again, sometimes she would wait for her husband's arrival in a cheerful mind and would consider herself fortunate about it. Like the reflection found in the drops of rainwater during the monsoon, like the sudden flash of lightning in the summer afternoon, the radiance of which is visible for a few seconds, and the charming radiance of crystals which are fragile and momentary, the heart of a newly-wed woman could not remain steady at all. It was very difficult even for the gods to ascertain what feelings appeared in their minds.

I have mentioned earlier that Nilabrata's squandering habits were extremely strong. Because of that day by day he fell into such poverty that it became difficult for him to retain the servants who did the household duties. Hence Manottama had to do all the domestic chores herself. In spite of that one didn't notice her unhappy demeanour even for a single day. Only sometimes she would be a little morose thinking what was happening to her husband and how he would be able to spend the rest of his life in penury after doing away with all his luxurious habits. This made her remain silent and let out deep sighs occasionally. It made her family members and neighbours feel that

Manottama probably showed such despair due to her husband's foul language. Also, in reality a lot of her earlier glamour had faded away. After a few days passed by in this manner, one evening Nilabrata arrived in his bedroom. He saw Manottama lying alone on one side of the bed and deeply immersed in thoughts. He thought, if Manottama was not aware of his arrival, he would indulge in having a little fun. Deciding that, he secretly entered the inner chamber and said, "What dearest! Why didn't you sit down to read books today? Alas! What are you thinking at this hour in idleness? If you do not read books your mental faculties will fade out; should a learned woman spend her time in such an idle manner?"

Seeing her husband arrive all on a sudden, Manottama got up from the bed respectfully and said, "Dear Husband! In which way did you come today? Please sit down. Why do you make me feel guilty by entering the woman's chamber secretly? Seeing you today, I am remembering the great poet Bharatchandra Roy. The first arrival of the poet Sundar in the house of Bidya, the daughter of Birsingha, was exactly like this. I usually get to know even if ants come into the house, but I can swear and say that I did not know anything about your arrival."

Saying that Manottama gave out a loud laugh. After that she became composed and said, "Dearest, please take your seat. You are distressed because you were standing and I was lying down, so this is an offence on my part. Or is it an offence because I didn't get to know about it?"

Nilabrata said, "Dearest, why are you feeling so guilty? I am not blaming you, but just asking why you are not reading books."

Manottama replied, "My dear husband! You always get annoyed when you see me reading books, so today I had a kind of repulsion growing in my mind. Moreover, if there is no listener, can the speaker be satisfied by reading out things alone? That is why I was lying down and waiting for you. I am so fortunate today! My heart is filled with satisfaction in meeting you after such a long period of time. Just as the thirsty *chatak* bird prayed for rain, it was blessed instantly with cold water. As soon as the thirsty female partridge looked up at the moon, its pure light blessed her. Dear Husband! The stars have been favourable towards me today."

Nilabrata said, "Dearest! The manner in which you are expressing your emotions makes me feel you have some purpose or motive behind it and from your behaviour it seems you want to ask something. So, if my assumption is not false, ask me whatever you wish to know."

Getting the opportunity Manottama said, "Dear Husband, I have a suspicion in my mind. If you are not annoyed or dissatisfied, let me ask you and resolve my doubts."

Nilabrata kept silent for a while and said, "Good. Let me first hear your queries and then later I will try to answer whether they are justified or not. If they are justified, I will definitely try to address them."

Manottama said, "Dearest! Since you gave me the courage, I shall speak without fear. Please listen. Why do you get annoyed when I read books? It only reveals your malice or envy. And you spend all your time outside the house and do not enquire even for once how the household is being run. It is needless to add how this creates so much of disorder. As the patriarchal head of the family you know how things don't run in order if you do not show your interest. Why do you engage in such adverse activities? Also see how you have physically declined from your earlier condition and how lean and weak you have become. Also, the way you are living with lowly people and have involved yourself in vulgar activity and are squandering money unnecessarily, it would surely affect our domestic affairs and possibly result in various shortfalls. Are these beneficial for householders? That is why I am telling you, why do you behave in this unfavourable manner?"

Nilabrata smiled a little and said, "O my affectionate one! Why do you worry? Why do you harbour such evil thoughts? Why should I be annoyed in reading books? Where do you see my malice in your reading practices? But once in a while I do say, will you spend your entire life reading? When will you become successful in learning and start earning money with that knowledge? When will you discover more knowledge in your mental arena?"

"O, you intelligent one! Why do you have to worry whether I spend money for good causes or waste them for anything else? The way you know how to give advice and the manner in which you have become learned will make you definitely able to sort out all domestic problems in future. You will definitely be able to earn money in some way or the other. Is it for no reason that people are so keen to marry educated wives? Is it for no reason that people are so keen to become husbands of educated women? And is it for nothing that people desire to possess this valuable repertory? There is no doubt that surely, they see this as a positive attribute to benefit at some point of time or another. Fortunately, the way you have become so accomplished, it will definitely help me when I am in distress."

Manottama said, "Dear Husband! Why do you repeatedly make me feel guilty?" Saying this she bowed her head in shame. A little later she realized that it was not good to remain quiet after such virulent attacks and so decided to reply, "Dear Husband! Since you have encouraged me, why do I need to fear? I will tell you a few more things quite frankly. See, I am weak and feeble. There is no second instance of a destitute person in this world like a woman. The husband is the only support of these weak women. You are knowledgeable but even then, why do you unnecessarily make me feel like a culprit? Please consider the fact that women do not become educated in order to earn money. People are interested in educating the girl child so that she can learn the moral instructions as much as possible and thus help in looking after the family, nurture her children, supervise all domestic activities, serve her husband, and thus express interest in performing other activities as well."

Nilabrata said, "Dearest, you have made up your mind about performing domestic duties for women and only you know the way to rear up children and do other jobs. Do you think that the illiterate women of our neighbourhood cannot do them as expertly as you? Do they have to invite you to help them perform such duties?"

In this manner anger and inherent vices within him burst out like a volcano. It seemed as if venom was sprouting out from his mouth; his eyes were red as the hibiscus, and the heat of fire emanated from his nostrils. Under the influence of tremendous anger, he spoke, "Oh you indomitable woman! Do you think I will give in to your mesmerizing charm? You irreligious, sinful woman! Will you be able to lure me in your magical charms? Shame on the men who are slaves of women! Only fools will believe your words. Only foolish men will believe you and send their daughters to school in order to train them as prostitutes. Educating women in that manner and showing them the path to go astray are similar. Fie you! You are a thorn in the family lineage. Let this woman with evil motives stay on the streets."

Saying these words, he left the house. Manottama was totally surprized by seeing this undue temper of her husband. She thought what a deep trouble she was in. By looking at his mental makeup she realized it would never be possible to remove the permanent superstition embedded within his mind. One could not even dream about it. The benefit she received was being suspected and labelled as a wayward woman. "What a great reward I received in trying to give him some sane advice. What trouble! Nowadays the times are all reversed!"

O hard luck! The hearts of tender women are so suspect! Especially if she was not educated like Manottama, she would never be able to speak such harsh words to her husband. Therefore, this was ample proof both for the women as well as for men that the education of women was helpful for a great percentage and at the same time the uneducated and indiscreet men were creators of unnecessary trouble. But even after witnessing such terrible behaviour of her husband, Manottama was not disheartened to stop giving advice once again whenever she got a suitable opportunity. She would say, "Let me see if I can somehow change my husband's habits." Thinking about this she kept on expecting her husband's arrival and spent her time in a very morose condition.

Almost a fortnight was over and she could not enjoy the company of her husband and though mentally depressed about it, she was very cautious not to let anyone know about it. Whenever she was in close proximity with other people, she hid her inner thoughts with such expertise that no one could stop laughing after seeing her. But when there was no one near her, she would be engrossed in deep thoughts about the earlier incident. Sitting alone and helpless, a sort of touchiness and sensitivity arose in her mind. Resting her left cheek upon her left hand, she went on shedding tears continuously. When one saw the sweet figure of Manottama with haze in her tearful eyes, there arose a sort of inexpressible feeling. It seemed as if the full moon was covered by grey clouds and so the eyes, in the garb of a pair of partridges, were crying out in loud earnest. How pitiable was the heart of the young person who was averse to love? Their breasts were even harder than a rock. Not only were they satisfied by evading love, they even attempted to uproot the hope of love from the tender hearts of young maidens. It was a grave perversion to beckon the uprooted state of the women. There was almost no medicine for its remedy. Alas! What misfortune befell the spouse! What tragic state of conjugal love! Oh! When Manottama was deeply immersed in the insult meted out to her by her husband and was wondering about the future condition of her family, when pearl-like teardrops kept on falling continuously from her eyes, down her cheeks and flooded her heart, which stone-hearted person would not melt and sympathise after seeing her?

The sinful Nilabrata was really in evil company. Since the day he had the altercation with Manottama, he would spend his time by loitering in the woods. Occasionally he would come back to the locality and make undue complaints to the prostitutes about Manottama and try to get some affection out of them. Continuous starvation had made him physically weak and pale. One day, around two pm in the afternoon, when the heat of the sun had made the entire stretch of land barren as usual, and without any living beings around; when the east would sulk about the separation from the lover, and when the western sky stretched its hands to welcome the rays of the sun; when the entire sky seemed to be ablaze and seeing a mirage suddenly was also not impossible; under such circumstances Nilabrata sat alone in a leaf cottage that was located near a big tree within a forest, and occasionally he started thinking about his wife's behaviour. He imagined so many different kinds of mischief, sometimes evaluated Manottama's sane advice, and apprehended many more things. In the meantime, two of his earlier friends who had been travelling reached that place. In order to cool themselves from the heat, they stood in the shade of that tree next to Nilabrata's cottage and enjoyed the breeze. They were really surprised when they accidentally saw Nilabrata sitting inside the cottage deeply immersed in his thoughts. They started arguing among themselves the reason for Nilabrata's arrival in the forest. They said that it was probably because of this reason that he was not seen regularly. After such argument they addressed Nilabrata and asked him, "Friend! What is this? When have you come to this place without informing us? Sitting here alone in this desolate forest, what are you thinking? Is it a suitable place for you to stay here in this lonely forest and also in this tremendous heat? Your health has deteriorated so much that if you were seen all of a sudden no one would recognize you. Seeing your appearance and your demeanour it seems you have been inflicted by a serious thought. After seeing you in this condition we cannot keep our minds still. The bleak face of our dear friend is distressing us even more than the tremendous heat of the afternoon sun. Nilabrata was startled after he looked outside but at the same time felt rather fortunate after the arrival of his friends. For some time, he remained speechless. A little later he addressed them and said, "Friends! Where were you travelling? From where have you come and where shall you go?"

They replied, "Friend! We had ventured to travel in the forest and have arrived at this place by chance. We had no other desire to travel elsewhere. Now your depressed appearance is giving us a lot of pain. Quickly narrate about yourself and satisfy us."

Nilabrata said, "Friends! You all rest in this place for a little while and I will tell you the entire story of my misfortune from the beginning to the end. But what will you do by listening to it? But if you feel that you need to hear it, then listen."

After the three of them sat down together, Nilabrata said, "Friends! You know how miserably I am spending my time since I married that sinful woman."

Hearing that they were alarmed. Oh! He had gone that far! "Friend, what happened after that?"

Nilabrata said, "Since my marriage my mind has been completely shattered and so I do not like anything else. On top of it, that detestable woman constantly tries to teach me morality. She asks me to get rid of bad company and for every little thing she brings out a printed book and starts reading from it. And her audacity is also not negligible. She tells me, "Dear Husband! Come and see what ethical lessons have been imparted here." Within her talk she tries to tell me that female education is very helpful; children get excellent education from their mother; child marriage is a great sin, and widow remarriage is approved by the *shastras*. Listening to all that rubbish I got disgusted and anger started to rage through my whole body.

As it is the mind of a woman naturally tends towards evil ways and on top of that, learning to read from all those destructive texts, will we be saved? If someone who is easily fickle-minded goes on having those ideas, shall we be relieved? That is why I am so depressed and worried. On that night, she clearly told me, "Why are you always averse to studies?" Do you consider this to be a little impertinence of a woman? I have also given her a suitable reply. I said, "No, why will I be disturbed? You wear a turban and go to the *kuthi* – the estate office, that is my complete desire." I am full of sorrow because that is not happening soon."

The two friends smiled slightly and replied, "Friend! You have not said anything wrong. Nowadays things have become like this. Many men are now spending sleepless nights in promoting the development of female education. They are now counted and respected among men. Their only devotion seems to be the development of female education, implementation of widow remarriage, stop the marriage tradition of the *kulins,* and prevent child marriage. Some people are squandering all their reputation, prestige and wealth in trying to get a widow remarried and mould his domestic household. Some people cannot even sleep in peace at night because the ritual of *kulin* marriage is still prevalent. They only know what they are gaining by this. Their words seem to have turned prophetic now. Even though they might not be so, they want to call them the dictates of the *shastras* according to whatever they have understood. And if we give them instances from the *shastras* and say that some words cannot be proved, even those would be against the *shastras*. So, I think, recently Manu and other thinkers who are appearing in the

39

world once again are themselves disowning their earlier dictums and rectifying them. There is no doubt that these are the faults of the times. Anyhow, friend! Is it for this reason that you have started living in the forest? Fie! You are a coward. Can any married wife be so strong? There is a saying called "*Praharena Sumangalam*," meaning beating brings in good results. If ghosts can be brought under control by beating, can't human beings be done so?"

Nilabrata said, "What you said is the best. Today if she comes to dictates terms to educate me, I shall beat her and teach her a lesson. Today I will do what is there in my mind."

The friends said, "Friend! See! There is another work to be done. You will do as we have instructed you to do, but that superstitious lady will never be of a simple nature. Since she has received some education, it will be extremely difficult to bring her back to her natural self. So, according to us, marrying a woman from a respectable family and with trustworthy manners once again will be the best for you. Then there will be no problems with you anymore. It will be like putting some salt upon a leech. Also, we have heard that if you have a second wife, the earlier one will also mend her manners. If the older wife sees the husband loving and caressing the newly married wife, she will start feeling jealous and that might cure her of her nature. That is why many learned men consider it to be the greatest medicine for changing the nature of a woman.

So, please marry a second time."

Nilabrata said, "Good. Let's see!" Later he decided to marry once again.

While all these conversations were going on, the sun went down. The entire place was engulfed in darkness. Along with his friends, Nilabrata departed towards his home. The almighty has created different people with different kinds of faculties and it is his well-thought out and planned strength. Only he alone knew how many people were practicing their strategies with the strength of his eternal glory. That same almighty has also given rise to mental deformity that is beyond the understanding of human intelligence. There is no record of how many people with different attributes and who do not possess any special faculties that he has blessed and also encapsulated them with a web of illusions. So many people have learnt to speak eloquently and so state real things as unnecessary, and unnecessary things as genuine in such a manner that it is not impossible to believe them. Nilabrata's friends tried to establish these ideas about the evil aspects of this country in such innovative lectures that all inexperienced people would feel that it was not the mission of the reformers to do away with child marriage and other evil practices. In reality, there were hundreds of places in the *shastras* where antidotes for such superstitions had been provided.

On the other hand, Manottama completed all her household duties before sunset and then

41

entered the kitchen. At that time one or two neighbour's daughters and a couple of five or six-year old boys came and assembled there. Manottama started cooking and at the same time telling them different stories with morals. The children kept on listening to her with full attention. In this manner, almost every day a few children would come and enjoy themselves for a couple of hours. On some days Manottama would entertain them further by reading out from an interesting book. She would explain to them in simple words the meaning of the words they could not understand. In this manner the mental horizon of several young children was being widened. On that day also, when she was reading out to them from a book, Nilabrata walked silently into the kitchen and saw Manottama engrossed in the reading. The girls were also attentively listening to her. Seeing that he said to himself, "What nuisance! She has still not been discouraged till today?"

He stood there secretly for some time but accidentally one girl caught sight of him. The girl said, "O, sister-in-law! See brother has come. See how he is hiding and secretly listening to our book reading." Manottama looked up and seeing her husband, gave a mild smile, closed her book and said, "Dear all, please wait for a while till I come back." Saying that, she got up. Nilabrata said, "So, what are you doing? Let this nuisance go away. You were reading the book quite comfortably, so go on reading. So, what did Sushila's father-in-law tell

Sushila?"

Manottama said, "Husband! Why do you ridicule like that? Come, let's go inside the house."

Nilabrata replied, "But why? Why do you have to welcome me? All those people are waiting for you, go and welcome them. I am leaving."

Manottama was ashamed and said, "Husband! Why do you make me feel ashamed? I become very sad for that. Sister-in-law Binodini of that house and the children of the new aunt had arrived. You were also not at home and so I was reading the first section of the Sushila story. What is the fault in doing so?"

Nilabrata said, "No, why will it be a fault? You were reading and I came and disturbed it, so the fault is mine. Weren't you really sad for that?"

Manottama laughed and said, "Dearest! I shall never be able to compete with you in words. Also, it is unnecessary to carry on such a debate. It is my fault, so please forgive me."

After such a conversation, Manottama went to make arrangements for dinner. All the young boys and girls who had assembled also took leave of Manottama and went back to their respective houses. After Nilabrata finished his dinner, Manottama had her food and went to the bedroom. She thought she would give him advice once again that night and wait and see what happens. After speaking about different things when it was quite late at night, Manottama said, "Husband! Whenever I propose to speak to you about any domestic affair, you get annoyed and leave. But how can I rest in peace? The few friends you have gathered will not leave you till you turn to be one like them. Even the prostitutes are draining all your natural and good attributes. You are spending your days and nights in lowly company. You cannot tolerate a single word spoken to you. You cannot even consider how beneficial it would be for you if you spent a fraction of time in doing some noble deeds from the base activities you enjoy yourself doing all the while. How long will a domestic man survive if he goes on indulging in such unlimited expenditure? Please get rid of your bad company and your spendthrift habits otherwise this household cannot be run in a decent manner. By speaking these words, I too in a way have indulged in criticising my husband. My advice is like being a glow worm and asking the moon to spread light. Or maybe it is not as bad as that because in the last month of Kartick, there was a discussion of *The Mahabharata* in the priest's house. I have heard that in the Aadi Parva, when Shakuntala, the daughter of Viswamitra, who was brought up by the sage Kanwa, went to meet her husband King Dushmantya, he could not recognize her as his wife due to the curse of sage Durbasha, and hence refused her. At that time Shakuntala had said, "Maharaj! I have heard that all the people belonging to the Puru dynasty were sincere and honest. But how come you had promised to take care and responsibility of the unfortunate woman when you married her and now are evading the truth? And how come you are diverting from it? So, Dear King! This sort of falsehood is not worth your name or your lineage." So, dear Husband! I am also saying that you too are bound by the truth of marriage with this ill-natured woman. Please do what you think is suitable for our bondage to remain intact, and also please pardon my audacity."

Saying these words, Manottama covered herself with the loose end of her saree and kept quiet. Enlivened with anger, Nilabrata said, "Yes, I have committed a great sin and am evading the truth. At the time of our wedding, you too had promised to remain true and since you are not uneducated like me, you can look after me for the rest of my life. You evil woman with loose morals! You go on regularly looking down upon me and imparting advice. Aren't you ashamed?" Saying that, just as a monkey flares up after being stung by a scorpion, he became restless in a similar manner and kicked Manottama. Alas! What a strange expression of anger! What strange reaction a person with indomitable anger has! What excellent power is expressed by the all-destroying illiterate man! Also, what heartless, selfish and insensitive men become the root cause for all this trouble. Praise be to anger! Under your influence, what wrong deeds can human beings not perform?

Through this sort of anger so many people have deserted their well-loved and doting sons, this anger has made so many people kill their respected parents, and it is through this anger that so many people have sinned by committing suicide! So, this sort of a behaviour by Nilabrata was not so strange. All these vices rule upon illiterate people and those devoid of common sense with similar force. Nilabrata therefore seethed in anger and after kicking and rebuking Manottama, left the house that very night.

Later, on the advice of his friends, he went and married a woman called Bimalprabha and began to spend his time in great happiness. This same Nilabrata had earlier been determined not to marry at all. Since he married the second time, he started spending time with his new bride entirely in the *antahpur*, the inner chambers. He was almost acting according to her dictates, even sleeping and eating with her permission. Earlier the same person would utter, "Shame on men who serve women." Now it was no longer a crime to come under the dictates of this kind of a lady. If the wife was of a tender nature and intelligent, there was no loss in giving her due respect and listening to her. But nothing was good in the extreme. This second wife of Nilabrata was very shrewd and jealous by nature. She would express her jealousy towards Manottama and would also speak to Nilabrata with sarcasm and disrespect but the saddest part of this was that in spite of that, Nilabrata's spendthrift nature, his binges of drinking and his enjoyment with the prostitutes were neither curtailed nor supressed. Instead, it went on increasing day by day.

In due course of time Bimalprabha became pregnant and at an auspicious moment gave birth to a male child. Seeing his son's face, Nilabrata started shedding tears of joy. Even though it was beyond his means, he promised to give the poor people and orphans whatever they demanded. In a way, his charity knew no bounds. He did not even pay heed to Bimalprabha's requests. Praise be to this unnatural love! There is nothing in the world you cannot do. As it is Bimalprabha was possessed by the female attributes of jealousy and to add to that she thought that by giving birth to a son, she had become the most endearing object of her husband. All this made her swell with pride. All the while she would never set her feet on the ground. Indulgent women thought no end of themselves by lording over the other wives and trying to retain their charm over their husbands. For Bimalprabha who was on the one had receiving her husband's devotion and expressing jealousy for the co-wife on the other and then giving birth to a son – all these were nothing strange to her. She would often speak to Manottama in such a derogatory manner that one felt sad even to describe it. Actually, if all these jealous and illiterate attributes were found in women, it was easily understood how far they could go. Manottama was not annoyed even for a day because there was a co-wife or that she had given birth to a son. On the other hand, she considered the co-wife as her own sister and her son as her own. She also did not neglect to pay due respect to her husband. Like earlier times, she went on serving him, would be present in front of him during his meals, and would always obey all the commands that were given to her. A least bit of exception or negligence was never noticed on her part. Why would it be so? Just because she was a woman did not necessarily mean that she had to be jealous and full of malice. There were so many instances of women who had behaved generously with their co-wives. Kaushalya, the wife of King Dasarath, had given to Sumitra, Lakshman's mother, half of the rice pudding she was given by her husband. Both of them shared such cordial relationship. Debjani, the daughter of Sukracharya, had tortured and insulted Kumari Sharmistha to such a great extent, but in spite of that she never misbehaved with her. Because of that the daughter of the acharya had given a curse to Jajati that he would turn old and decrepit but even then, the daughter of the king of demons did not misbehave with the daughter of Bhrigu. In a similar manner, Manottama showed endurance and kept on serving her husband and behaved well with her co-wife and her son. Seeing that, both Bimalprabha and Nilabrata believed that Manottama was serving them probably because she was greedy of some fortune, but in reality, that was not her intention. Just because the planet Rahu engulfs the moon, does it mean that her brightness can be permanently deleted? When the stalks of grain are heavy with the produce, can the wind keep it from stooping down and make it face upwards again? Does an automatically sweet-natured object change its habits even though it is repeatedly hurt by men? If a stalk of sugarcane is cut into several pieces by a weapon, does its sweetness go away? Does the sandalwood tree situated on the Malabar mountain range in South India lose its fragrance because it is encircled by snakes? Does the sandalwood lose its fragrance when it is repeatedly being rubbed? And does the very beautiful gold lose its beauty because it is repeatedly burnt in the fire? Just as it was impossible for these objects never to lose their natural attributes, similarly it was impossible for Manottama who was educated and peaceful by nature to bring in shame to the family by discarding her true nature, even if it meant death for her. Otherwise she would have never tolerated Nilabrata's constant rebukes and kicks. Hence it was useless fearing such a possibility.

In the meantime, Bimalprabha's son turned four months old. During this period the women from neighbouring houses would come and praise the boy's handsome features. He would also be passed on from one person's lap to another and would gratify the visitors. Seeing their son's sweet smile, the parents were also filled with happiness. Manottama was five months pregnant when Bimalprabha's son was born. According to local customs and beliefs, she did not touch any item that was used by the new born child. This resulted in a lot of debate that she did that out of jealousy. Basically, Manottama was not that sort of a woman who would be jealous. Even listening to such a thing was sacrilege for her. When Bimalprabha's son was five months old, Manottama gave birth to a baby boy. Nilabrata heard about it and though he was sincerely happy he could not express his happiness as he had done when Bimalprabha's son was born fearing his younger wife. The same Nilabrata who would feel insulted if Manottama gave him advice now received similar lectures from Bimalprabha each morning. She would go on casting invectives upon him even for very minor things. The same advice imparted by Manottama would prick him like a bomb shell but now his same body had to endure all the invectives of his new wife. Alas! Illiterate men were so dangerous! Shuttling between his two wives like the spindle in the cloth weaving machine, Nilabrata was similar to the foolish people who sinned and enjoyed themselves by marrying several times. The same Nilabrata who earlier never stayed in the house either at daytime or at night was now living permanently in the *antahpur,* the inner chambers. This was of course not a matter of complaint. Though I had mentioned earlier that it was not harmful to stay under the control of a woman with good attributes, it does not mean that anything was good in excess.

One day when Manottama was sitting with her son on her lap at the entrance of the secluded child birthing room, Nilabrata chanced to pass that way. Seeing his son, he suddenly stopped and looked at him for a while. While enjoying the beauty of his son's physical features, he went on looking cautiously all around him. Oh, how fortunate a man was with a son! Down the ages people without sons were unable to feel the pleasure and delight of looking upon the face of a son. The immense happiness that could be obtained at the birth of a son was often marred if there was a person in the family who was jealous and full of malice. The feeling of savouring immortal nectar was then countered with the shower of poison. In spite of feeling happy and fortunate in gaining a son, Nilabrata was also shrinking in fear of Bimalprabha when suddenly she arrived there and said, "Husband! What are you doing there? By standing like a mad man at the entrance of the child-birthing room, what are you staring at? You are not even moving your eyelids. Standing there like a painted picture, what are you looking at?"

Nilabrata was taken by surprise and said, "What? What will I see? I haven't seen anything much."

Bimalprabha smiled and said, "Haven't you seen anything much? You were staring at the child-birthing room."

Nilabrata was scared and said, "Dearest! Nothing much. But this son is not that bad and I was watching him."

"Who said he is bad?" Bimalprabha replied. "But now come aside, I need to have some special discussions with you."

Hearing these words, Nilabrata turned around like a buffalo with a noose in his pierced nose. Manottama let out a deep sigh and went inside the child-birthing room.

Bimalprabha said, "Husband! The time for my son's *annaprasan*, the rice-eating ceremony has arrived. For that some little things need to be done. You will have to invite all the relatives and acquaintances from my father's village and also all the people from our society. Pitchers of oil have to be distributed in the entire village, and seeking the long life of our son, a special kind of pulse and fish will also have to be distributed. The ceremony of collecting water from the river accompanied by procession of lights and illumination has to be done, at night one group will recite the *panchali*, that is Bengali poems chanted with devotion, and there will be two contingents of courtesans to dance. Besides that, you will have to do all the other rituals that are customary in your family."

Listening to all her demands, Nilabrata was deeply worried. He didn't know what to do; knowing his own condition he understood that it was not very easy to satisfy his wife's demands but he could not say anything out of fear and hence kept quiet. Bimalprabha gave a false smile and said, "Husband! It is not surprising that you are keeping quiet about my son's annaprasan ceremony. If it was the annaprasan ceremony of Manottama's son, then by this time even Basuki, the mythical snake king would be ashamed by looking at your face. There would be no limits to your pleasure. He is just a fifteen-day old child and you were awestruck at seeing him. What more shall I see in future?"

Nilabrata was ashamed and broke his silence by saying, "My dearest! Why do you unnecessarily rebuke me? I was absent-minded because I was trying to finalise the auspicious date for the annaprasan ceremony. Otherwise I am even willing to lay down my life in order to satisfy your desires. Moreover, it is especially the ceremony for my son who is dearer to me than my own life and for that I will not refuse to do things that are impossible to be done."

Manottama heard his words from inside the child-birthing room and thought, "Oh! He seems like King Dasarath and partly an avatar."

Instilling confidence in his beloved wife in such a manner, Nilabrata went out of the *antahpur* and started to think how he would raise funds for the occasion. He went to a trader friend called Harananda and loaned an amount of five thousand rupees at an interest of ten percent. The preparations for the annaprasan ceremony continued in full swing. Manottama thought, "How terrible! How could I bring this colossal wastage to my husband's ears? How can I tactfully make him understand; or will making him understand be of any use? I can see what is going to happen. Just as a lamp flickers and brightens up before it extinguishes itself, this incident would be similar to that. His decadence has turned to become like the all-engulfing fire. There isn't much time left for him to be ruined. Now what could be done? The manner in which the people of this country make the child-birthing room resemble an unholy place akin to hell, they would never come here at the cost of their lives. If by chance they come close to the room or near the new born child, they instantly go and bathe in the Ganges to purify their bodies once again. Also, it is impossible for me to get permission to enter the other parts of the house. If I don't abide by these local customs and enter the house, I will be immediately chided as a destroyer of religious beliefs. The house will have to be purified once again by worshipping Lord Shiva in a special ritual and by offering *tulsi* leaves. So now what should I do? On the other hand, there is still time for the sixth month to be completed and according to tradition, six full moons have not yet gone by. Maybe by that time I will be able to go out of this place." Manottama spent her time in such thoughts.

In due course of time when one month was over, she and her son came out of the child-birthing room and after fulfilling the bathing rituals, entered the main house once again.

Finding some spare time, that same night she called Nilabrata and said, "Husband! This audacious woman wants to speak to you about something today. If you kick me again for that, I shall consider it as praise. Even receiving rebuke for it will be my reward. That too is the best fortune for women. That day while I was in the child-birthing room, I overheard that the younger wife was requesting you to indulge in some unnecessary expenditure to celebrate the annaprasan ceremony. You also gave in to her demands and consented to everything. Now if I say anything about it, you will think just the opposite and create more trouble. But my husband, one is never averse to *amrita*, the holy nectar. But now the times and conditions are such that one has to consider them. It is always essential for a domestic person to consider present circumstances and then take necessary decisions. By merely shutting one's eyes and spending lavishly with both hands cannot make a person be called rich. Hence, at this time it is wise to spend with limitations in a way that there is no criticism in society and the rituals are completed according to the dictates of our standard *kulin* tradition. I think there is no need to waste money unnecessarily on *panchali* performance, dances by tawaifs, illumination etc. Also, the ritual of going to the river in a procession is nothing great. Moreover, I have never seen anyone perform such dances and tamasha for an annaprasan ceremony. If someone does it, there is no doubt that he is a spendthrift. Now it is up to you to decide what you will do."

Hearing all these words, Bimalprabha started screaming like the untimely roar of thunder and said, "Here you! How come you are giving moral instructions to the husband? So, do you want to stretch out your ten hands and consume everything by yourself? Don't I have any mortal desires? People say that if one is educated, she doesn't have jealousy or hatred but I see the exact reverse in your nature."

Manottama said, "Sister! I had already anticipated that you would say things like that and that is why I have not said anything secretly to our husband. I saw you there decorating your house and that is why I called him to say these words. I can swear and state that if I don't consider your son equal to mine, and if I have spoken these words out of jealousy, or if I have some other intentions in my mind, then the almighty god will judge it. I should never become fortunate at any time. What can I say sister! This is my fate. Even if I speak ordinary words, I get unnecessarily accused of evil ways. I knew beforehand that my pure word will bear poisonous fruit. Anyhow, I should not have spoken them. Now you can do whatever you decide to be best for you. I have nothing more to say."

Bimalprabha said, "Yes, that's the best. Keep your holy words aside for now. You can use them for your son's annaprasan ceremony. Why do you add poison now?"

Nilabrata also dismissed Manottama's words and left the place in disgust. Manottama understood the implications and sat there with her head bent low. Seeing her dejected state, Bimalprabha also laughed and left.

The preparations for the annaprasan went on. Everyone was pleased and it was noticeable in their appearance. Holy chants were echoed from everyone's mouth. The whole town was abuzz with sound and it made the passers-by inquisitive. Spending five thousand was not an ordinary affair. The priests with holy mud of the Ganges anointed on their forehead, shawls with Lord Krishna's name printed on them covering their bodies, and with silk dhotis around their waist arrived at Nilabrata's house chanting praises in loud voices. The annaprasan was still seven days away. The auspicious day was finalised on the following Monday. The priests decided to stay there for those five days and began their rituals of chanting prayers. Some took the responsibility of distributing the invitation cards, some started procuring the required food items, some went to select the dancers, some to book the holy scripture from where chants would be conducted, some to pay an advance to the musicians, some to supervise and dictate terms to the jewellers, some to distribute oil, and some became busy arranging for the illumination. In this manner hundreds of men went about doing hundreds of jobs. There was no limit for the preparations.

By Saturday evening there arose divided

factions among them. It was a division among the Kayasthyas. A few landlords were also occasionally seen. All of them were entitled to receive holy offerings. They were engrossed in the idea that they were the gurus and need not bother about anything and also could do things as they wished. Anyhow, on the whole this factionalism was not bad. People like Ghosh, Basu, Mitra, Dutta, Shiv, Goswami and others got together. Almost everyone had a stint of grey hair on their head and almost everyone carried a hookah in their hands. Some Brahmins, with a tuft of hair on their shaven heads, carried a box of crushed tobacco in their hands. In fact, if all these people were not decked up differently, the factionalism among them would not be present so colourfully. It seemed as if a group of people had gathered there to present the songs of the Ramayana. The factionalism did not reveal itself until all the important persons of the village gathered together. They did not pay heed to the opinion of the ordinary people for all noble work they had done and also did not think it to be necessary. The gathering had been arranged in an open place. The leaders were seated in the centre with the audience surrounding them on all sides. No one know how things would turn up – whether it would resemble the slaying of Abhimanyu, the fight of Mahishasur, or the killing of the great Ravana. Some said that Tarini Mitra from the next neighbourhood was a sympathizer of widow remarriage, so he should be socially ostracized. Someone said that the daughter of one Mr Ghosh had got married to a groom of the Dutta lineage, so he had lost his caste and hence could not be invited. Someone said, one daughter of Ramananda Basu had remained unmarried till the age of twelve and then got married. Therefore, it was their duty to boycott him, while another great man retorted, "Listen, Ramananda babu did not retain the prestige of the *kulins* in that marriage. There might be some special reason behind it. So, he has to be socially boycotted from our caste." Someone else added that no one should go to Nilabrata's house because his father-in-law Yogananda has a daughter who is educated and one of his sons, aged sixteen years, still remains unmarried. Hearing that, one great leader, Shiromani Bhattacharya took some snuff and stated, "What? Getting educated in spite of being a woman? And a sixteen-year old son still unmarried? Then we cannot drink water from their hands. Especially, most of the women who get educated are prostitutes." Hearing that someone said, "Sir! The daughter of Yogananda who has got educated is actually the same woman whom Nilabrata has married."

Just at that moment Nilabrata arrived there at the gathering. Taken aback, the Shiromani put some more snuff into his nose and said, "What! This gentleman? He is Nilabrata? Then –?" Mitraja said, "Then, Bhattacharya Mahashoy?" Shiromani scratched his head and said, "Well, it is not such a great fault in getting a woman educated, it is not getting the sixteen-year-old son married that is a sin." Hearing that some people started laughing, some got up in anger and were about to leave the meeting, whereas others followed them and begged at their feet. There was a great chaos and at that time there was no certainty as to who fell upon whom, who beat whom, or who listened to whom. The whole place was choc-a-bloc with people. Nilabrata tried to pacify everybody. It was a funny scene to watch.

After all the factionalism ended, Nilabrata ostracized some people completely, some partly, got some people totally banished from their caste, and at the auspicious moment performed the annaprasan ceremony of his son. According to the locally prevalent custom, each invited guest blessed the child with money according to his individual means. Because the son had been born from the womb of his beloved wife, Nilabrata named him Priyabrata. Alas! What a terrible nature of the so-called leaders of the society was revealed, exposing how their jealousy, hatred, and shrewdness was always ingrained within them. Although all the people belonging to the different factions had their personal vested interests, chaos occurred in some groups even without any intention on the part of the leaders. It seemed that it occurred just for the simple reason of creating pure brawl and hurting the minds of the people and nothing else. Actually, the main intention of this group was to create conflict, quarrel and egotism.

In this instance, four issues were noticeable – getting widows remarried, educating the girl child, not accepting the status of the daughter's marriage, and not getting a son married by the age of sixteen. All these were considered by the above-mentioned social leaders as great disaster and steps leading to sin. They considered all these things as great deviation from religion. It was not a trifle affair to regret. The way in which the above-mentioned group considered widow remarriage, women's education and boys above sixteen years remaining bachelors as tragic and detestable ideas, if they showed even one percent interest in their abhorrence towards abortion, adultery, giving respect to marriage, (selling of daughters) etc, we cannot say how beneficial it would be. But unfortunately, in a way they were helping people for their sinful attitude towards female education, prevention of child marriage, widow remarriage etc. Alas! What disaster has arrived! Is Bharatvarsha till now suffering in the poor condition she has fallen in? To see that Bharatvarsha which for centuries faced so many hundreds of famines and yet had ascended the peak of civilization was now a distant dream. We must even thank the citizens for remembering the way in which the earlier kings in this country were charitable and noble minded. Indian people had turned civilized a long time ago. But what a pitiable condition of our motherland we are witnessing now. Those who were uncivilized like wild tribes till some time ago, those people of England have now come to Bharatvarsha as civilized beings. Those who till some time ago did not have any knowledge what to eat and drink, now that same uncivilized English race is educating the people of Bharatvarsha and the people of Bharatvarsha are imitating their civilization and practicing it. Even now they have not gained any realization. Laziness and sleep have now engulfed us. The people of Bharatvarsha who are following these wrong deeds and those who cannot free themselves from the grip of heart-rendering superstitions, it cannot be said that all of them are foolish. Most of them are educated and knowledgeable. But what about that? Sometimes they indulge in horrible deeds and by that they put a scar of disrepute over the name of being knowledgeable. There is no longer any fame for knowledge. This is also an eternally shameful subject. Anyhow, it is our duty to know what Nilabrata's condition is at present.

Meanwhile, Manottama's son turned six months old. Manottama thought, 'tomorrow is the date of annaprasan for the child. If I don't mention about it now, then jealousy and sorrow would be expressed. If I say that the annaprasan ceremony has to be held, it would raise the indulgence of the co-wife and if I say that the annaprasan is indispensable, then the husband would be ashamed about what people would say and so he would be forced to take loan once again. That was also not desirable.' Now, which path should she adopt? In the end she decided to say, "Husband! The time for the son's annaprasan has arrived, so what are your orders?" Yes, that seemed all right. She would say that. Accordingly, she addressed Nilabrata in the evening and said, "Husband! The new son will complete his sixth lunar month a few days later. Now what do you want to do?" Nilabrata did not offer a reply. Bimalprabha heard that and came out and said, "Why? At that time, you had spoken about our condition several times, now why are you saying all this? So, sister, you see everyone has the same desires. You should think about yourself before speaking about others."

Manottama replied, "Sister! Your desires have really been fulfilled. I am not sincerely sorrowful because of my son's annaprasan."

Bimalprabha said, "And what will you do by being sad? This time is not suitable for celebrating his annaprasan." Nilabrata could not utter a single word even then. So, Manottama's son's annaprasan did not take place. Manottama bent her head low and said, "Sister! (then addressing Nilabrata) Husband! Listen. It is not written anywhere that if you have a son his annaprasan ceremony has to be held; but since it is our custom, I mentioned it once. If my husband ignores it even after that, why should I complain? You all bless him and with the blessing of the elders he will naturally live a long life."

This was how quarrels began, but with Manottama's unconcern, it was nipped in the bud. If the educated woman did not have such virtues, why would people worship education so much? Manottama behaved with equal justice towards her own son, her co-wife's son, her co-wife and her husband. By looking at her it seemed that she loved her co-wife and her son even more than her own self or her own son, let alone serving her husband. One should infinitely praise her for paying respect to such a characterless and ill-natured husband.

One day Manottama thought, it was all right that her son did not have his annaprasan ceremony, never mind, but he needed to be named. Thinking about that she smiled and picked up the son from the cradle and made him sit on her lap. Caressing his head and body she said, "Son, always follow the path of truth. You should never be attracted to falsehood." Saying that, she blessed him and named him Satyabrata. As the moonbeam ventures towards the full moon, the boy also started growing up naturally.

In due course of time, Bimalprabha gave birth to two daughters and Manottama to one daughter with good attributes. All the three girls were pretty. The two daughters of Bimalprabha were known as Hemprabha and Swarnaprabha. Manottama's daughter was named Hemlata. As the children started speaking, they made their parents happy. Later when they started walking, they would roam around between one house and another. They entertained their parents and neighbours with their baby talk.

So, everyone loved them and they were not neglected anywhere. The pundits who wrote the *shastras* have said that during pregnancy the mental condition of the parents gets reflected exactly in the nature of the children. If the parents suffer from any incurable disease, the children are bound to get them. Details about this can be explained at any opportune moment. Now let us speak about the qualities found in serving the husband.

One day, Manottama's father Yogananda visited his son-in-law's house after a long time. When Manottama heard about her father's arrival, she eagerly sent a message asking him to come to the inner chambers of the house. Yogananda went there and asked Manottama to come near him. Manottama came and welcomed him and offered him a seat. She carefully brought whatever was available in the house, sat next to him with tearful eyes and said, "Father! Is everything all right at home? Are you keeping well? Is everyone in the village fine too? Oh, I haven't seen you for a long time and so seeing you today I cannot hold my tears." Saying that, she covered her face with the loose end of her sari and went on crying. Yogananda got anxious and wiping the tears from his daughter's eyes, said, "Dear Manottama! Don't cry. You are in your husband's home and that makes us sufficiently happy. Where are your children?" Manottama rubbed her eyes and said, "Father! They have just gone out to play. Please sit down, I am calling them." Saying that, she came out quickly and asked a woman, "Here you! My father has come. Go and see where the children have gone and call them." Since Manottama was so sweet-natured, how could anyone refuse her? She instantly went and brought Priyabrata, Satyabrata, and the three sisters along with her. Manottama held all their hands and took them to her father saying, "Father! These children are paying obeisance to you. Please bless them. This is my eldest son, this the youngest, and these are my three daughters." She introduced them in this way. Yogananda said, "Oh, what beauty! What sweetness! Let God bless them with long lives. But daughter, I had heard that you had only one son and one daughter. So, when were these five children born?" Manottama replied politely, "These three are the children of my co-wife who is like my sister, but they are always with me. They love to spend their time with me and do not care much about their biological mother." Yogananda said, "Yes. Children always love to stay in that place from where they receive affection." Saying that he gave them money individually and blessed them with a long life. Manottama said, "Father! I pray for you to please say that again." The children were happy and danced around by saying "We have got money!" Then they started running away while giving casual glances to see whether their mother was following them. Manottama laughed and said, "Father! The impossible has been achieved. They are very restless and cannot sit in one place for a couple of seconds." Saying that she started chasing them. The two boys also laughed and said, "Ma is coming" and then ran away. Drops of sweat started falling from Manottama's brow till she managed to get hold of them after a lot of effort. They started crying and following their mother. The three girls on the other hand sat next to Yogananda and played while delighting him with a few occasional words.

Manottama arrived there with the two boys and said, "Father! I have grown very tired after running behind these little boys. See how I am sweating profusely." Yogananda said, "Daughter, what can you do? Boys by nature are restless. You can realize how much trouble you have to bear if you have children." Manottama smiled, bent her head in shame, and started wiping her sweat with the loose end of her sari. A little later, Yogananda said once again, "Daughter! Just because I could not attend Priyabrata's annaprasan ceremony due to some other engagement, you did not invite me for Satyabrata's annaprasan out of that offended state of mind?" Manottama replied with tears in her eyes, "Father! My Satyabrata's annaprasan was not held in a ceremonious way. Just some time before that a lot of expenses were incurred during Priyabrata's ceremony and that too there has been some loan also. Everyone in the house wanted a lot of celebrations to be held for Satyabrata's annaprasan as well, but I disagreed because I thought taking more loan was not right. That is why nothing was done. But you bless him so that he lives a long life."

Yogananda said, "You need not say that." After debating within his mind about the practical wisdom of his own daughter, he said, "Dear Manottama! If there is difficulty in your family because of the loan taken, and I have also heard from various sources that you are not as solvent as before, wouldn't it be nice if you went and stayed in my house for some time? I am requesting you, so what is the fault in that?" Manottama bent her head and said, "Father! What kind of an order are you giving me? What is the difficulty in my own household? And even if there are difficulties, is it feasible for any wife devoted to her husband to desert him at this difficult time? If I went just because you feel that I am suffering here, it is in no way justified that I go. Even if she has to suffer terrible hardship, a wife should never desert her husband because he has fallen into hard times. Father! On such a day a few years ago, a *bhairabi,* a woman mendicant, had arrived at my father-in-law's house. She had never come earlier within any human locality. Like ancient sages, she lived in the deep forest. In earlier times the sages, men who undertook Vanaprastha, and persons detached from family life would often reside in the forest. They would not go begging from door to door or practice thievery like present day fortune tellers, mahantas and sages. One evening that *bhairabi* was delivering religious advice and we all went to listen to her.

My Satya was only two years old. It was there that I heard amazing religious dictates about wives being devoted to their husbands. Though it is rather shameful to discuss things related to a husband with you, but since I heard the advice, there is no harm in sharing it.

That lady mendicant had said that Sita, wife of Ramchandra, suffered a lot in the forest along with her husband but she never deserted him. Savitri, daughter of Aswapati, did not even hate her dead husband and with the strength of her religious beliefs, brought Satyaban back to life. Damayanti, daughter of King Bhima, was deserted by her husband and while travelling with King Nala in the forest, did not falter from her path even though she was extremely tired. Chinta, wife of Srivatsya, endured a lot of suffering when her husband was living in the forest and got him back once again by luck. Draupadi, daughter of King Panchala, suffered so much of hardship when she lived in the forest along with the five Pandava brothers. In the end, during the last year when they had to remain incognito, she fell into so much trouble when she worked as a servant in the land of the Matsyas, yet she never gave up the company of her husbands. In this manner the mendicant sang so many paeons for chaste wives who always adored their husbands. She even gave a strange example of how these sorts of devoted women were born even among the lower castes. When the king of Kalinga ordered the arrest and punishment of Kalketu in Gujarat, then

Fullara, the daughter of an archer had earnestly pleaded to the policemen, "You killer! You followers of the king. I am promising in the name of dharma that if you kill my living god before killing me, I will commit suicide in everyone's presence. O you witnesses! Believe in god! My resolution is that I do not have to see the end of my living husband while I am still alive." So, Father! Even when lower caste women turn out to remain devoted to their husbands, how can I, who belong to the bhadralok community, leave my husband in such hard times and go to my parent's house? Also, if there are hundreds of gratifying objects in the father's house, obeying the commands and serving the husband is desirable for all women. Even if there is no desire for physical comfort, it is against the dictates of the *shastras* to live forever in the father's house. Shakuntala, daughter of Menaka, was in a way a sage's daughter after leaving her home and her domestic duties, but even then, the great sage Kanwa sent her along with Gautami back to Hastinapur because it was her duty to serve her husband. Father! What other superior religion does a wife have except becoming a *patibrata*, a devotee of the husband? I cannot discard this great dharma of serving my husband even for a day. You please pardon me and do not make such a request. I remain guilty towards you, but please pardon me."

Yogananda said, "Child! Let my dissatisfaction be far away, today I have gained a lot of knowledge. You remain as happy as a queen, as pure as Sati and Savitri, and live a long life with your husband and children. You have proved yourself justified as a woman. Compared to my ten sons, you are my best daughter. I am feeling grateful being your father. Now let me take your leave."

Manottama touched her father's feet and said with tears in her eyes, "Father! Sometimes remember this sad daughter of yours."

Yogananda said, "Child! Spend your life without worries. I will sometimes come and see you." Saying that Yogananda got up from his seat. Manottama took him to Bimalprabha's house and said, "Father! This is my younger co-wife who is akin to my sister. She respects me a lot. It is because of her that I don't have to suffer anything."

Yogananda said, "It should be like that! Daughters from respectable families should be of such good character. He addressed Bimalprabha and said, "Mother! That both you sisters are residing so harmoniously makes me feel very satisfied indeed. Child! Spend a long domestic life with your son and children. I bless you. Become queens. I am seeing you as my own daughter. So, if you all remain happy, I will be happy too."

Bimalprabha thought to herself, "What nuisance! What rainfall in unusual times! As if everything will remain waiting for his words to come true."

Addressing Manottama and Bimalprabha,

Yogananda took leave of Nilabrata and set out for his own house. Manottama became engaged in household work. She called the sons and fed them. She started preparing her husband's meal. For a brief while she spoke to the other wives of the neighbourhood who had come to visit her. She did some art work. In this manner everyday she had her food after Nilabrata finished his meal and then went to sleep. She woke up again the next morning to undertake her regular duties. Her domestic rituals continued in this manner.

END OF THE FIRST SECTION

ABOUT THE TRANSLATOR

Somdatta Mandal is a former Professor of English at Visva-Bharati, Santiniketan. A recipient of several national and international fellowships and awards, she has been published widely. Her areas of interest include American Studies, Postcolonial Literature, Diaspora Studies, Culture Studies, and Translation. Apart from editing the first Indian English narrative published in 1835 entitled *A Journal of Forty-Eight Hours of the Year 1945* by Kylas Chunder Dutt, and the first Indian English drama published in 1831 entitled *The Persecuted* by Krishna Mohana Banerjea, she has also translated and edited the first Bengali travel narrative by a woman entitled *A Bengali Lady in England* by Krishnabhabini Das (1885). Mandal has also translated several other 19th and early 20th-century Bengali travel narratives and memoirs written by women and members of the Tagore family.

www.ingramcontent.com/pod-product-compliance
Lightning Source LLC
LaVergne TN
LVHW040211180726
843489LV00007B/2804